Violet's Finest Hour

By Alice Duggan
Illustrated by Harvey Stevenson

Lothrop, Lee & Shepard Books   New York

First Edition 1 2 3 4 5 6 7 8 9 10

Library of Congress Cataloging in Publication Data
Duggan, Alice, Violet's finest hour / by Alice Duggan ; illustrated by
Harvey Stevenson.
    p.   cm. Summary: Two young cats, unappreciated Violet and her
bragging friend Grim, use a magic flying cape to stop a gang of bank robbers.
ISBN 0–688–09456–2 [1. Cats—Fiction.   2. Robbers and outlaws—Fiction.
3. Flight—Fiction.]   I. Stevenson, Harvey, ill.   II. Title.
PZ7.D8784Vi   1991 [E]—dc20   91–52588 CIP AC

For David and Pete

Chapter One

There was vegetable soup for lunch. It had green things in it—soggy beans and okra. Violet stabbed them with her fork and scraped them off on her plate. No one noticed. She spread an extra layer of butter on her bread and chewed while she kicked the table. Thunk-thunk. Thunk-thunk. Thunk-thunk.

No one heard her. They were all too busy adoring her big sister Dagmar to notice anyone else.

"Dagmar, sweetheart, you look so nice," said Grandma.

Thunk-thunk, thunk-thunk, thunk-thunk-*bang* went Violet's foot in its worn-out cowboy boot.

"Doesn't she, though?" Mom was all

smiles. "That peach-colored dress is just lovely with her white fur."

Thunk-thunk, thunk-thunk, thunk-thunk-*bang.*

Violet stared at her sister, sitting there in her gleaming white fur. The new peach-colored dress just matched the heart-shaped spot between her ears. Dagmar could play the cello— perfectly. Dagmar danced divinely— everyone said so. She kept her room neat. When she ate, her whiskers stayed clean.

All the grown-ups were beaming. "That's our girl," said Dad. He didn't mean Violet.

Thunk-thunk, thunk, *bang!* THUNK, THUNK, *BANG!*

Suddenly, all eyes were on Violet. Once they were looking her way, they had just as much to say to her as they did to Dagmar.

"Stop that noise!" her father yelled, slamming his fist on the table.

"Eat your vegetables, dear, please," said her mother, frowning at Violet's mushy green pile.

"Heavenly days!" said her grandmother. "Look at your face! You haven't washed!"

Dagmar had something to say, too. "Look at that big greasy smear on your shirt! And all those burrs in your fur!"

Her mother yanked out a thick clump of burrs from behind Violet's ear. "Where have you been, dear?" she asked anxiously. Quickly, Violet stuffed her mouth full of bread. She gagged. She coughed. She swallowed a glass of water. She hurried away to wash. When she came back, they were talking about a cello recital.

She didn't tell them where she'd been. And she didn't eat her vegetables.

As soon as she and Dagmar had dried the last dish, as soon as the kitchen was empty and quiet, Violet slipped out the back door and raced through the garden. She was going to the dump. She knew the path by heart: under the giant catalpa, up the hill to the oak grove, into the woods. She pounded along the edge of a steep ridge until she hit the path that dropped down to the river. They wasted so much time just sitting around and eating! And talking—so much talking.

Violet leaped expertly from stone to stone, crossing the river. She had things to do, and no one to help her. Impatiently, she stopped to dump a pebble out of her boot, then strode off down the one track road.

Two turkey vultures circled over the dump, gliding on lazy wings. "Come down!" Violet called. "This is a great place. You can find all kinds of neat stuff." The vultures rolled and swayed in the far-off sky, growing smaller and farther away.

"Ugly old things," said Violet. She hurried around the towering piles of garbage. On the far side of the dump, a scrubby willow offered a thin shade. She had fenced in a little yard around it, using old tires. And close against the willow, lying on its side, was the old piano box that was her hideout. It was dark inside and cool. Violet flopped down on a sagging lawn chair to rest.

It was beautiful. It was private. It was all hers. No one told her to weed the petunias or practice the clarinet or fold the laundry while she was here. She could do whatever she wanted to, all by herself.

The shadows of willow leaves flickered over the dusty yard as she sprawled in her lawn chair and thought. This dump was bursting with treasure, all of it waiting for her. What fantastic luck she'd had already! She had a radio with all the knobs. A telephone with a long curly cord.

A big wooden spool to use for a table. And there was more out there, just for the taking. Violet leaped up, knocking the lawn chair over, and ran outside.

Prowling around the slopes near her hideout, she spotted a perfect chair. It was painted blue and only a little broken. She set it carefully outside the door to the box. The lawn chair could go right beside it, to make a pair. When she flipped the spool over, it landed neatly between the chairs. The phone and the radio looked just right on its top. "Nice!" she said. "We can sit outside."

Then Violet frowned at the cozy arrangement. Something was wrong. There was no "we." There was only Violet. Dagmar was home—probably reading a fashion magazine. Dagmar would say the dump was too dirty to play in. Dagmar was no use at all. Then who would sit in the blue chair? It made her feel crabby, looking at that empty chair. She looked away, toward the center of the dump where the tallest peak thrust itself into the blue spring sky. Mount Garbage, she called it.

"I'll bet there's some very good stuff up there," she said, "up at the very top." She vaulted over a TV set and scrambled up a truckload of tires. She crawled through a swamp of mattresses and then, just when she had a foothold near the top, a landslide of cardboard carried her down again, into a top-loading washing machine. "Wash–Rinse–Spin" read the dial on the washing machine. "Oh, drat," said Violet. She shook some coffee grounds out of her fur. "There's nothing here but garbage."

Then a patch of color caught her eye, a scrap of vivid purple. Violet pulled on it gently and it grew larger . . . it grew longer . . . it billowed in the breeze. It was a cape. A purple cape. It glowed like a jewel and it felt so soft to her touch that she shivered. It was magic; it couldn't be anything else. She tried it on. It fit perfectly. "Glory, glory," she breathed. "Glory be."

Violet knew instantly what the cape was for. She climbed on top of the washing machine and stood with her eyes shut tight. The right words, all she needed now were the right words. "Wash, spin, dry," she whispered. No, of course not. "Soar like a vulture," she tried. Nothing. "Fly like an eagle?" Her cowboy boots stayed rooted to the spot.

She wasn't a vulture or an eagle. She wasn't Dagmar, who was every-one's pet. With her rough gray fur and her rough ways, she was no one's pet. "And I don't care," she announced. "I am Violet."

Trees and garbage and sky rushed by. "I'm flying!" she gasped. She threw out her arms.

12

"Of course," she said, as she leveled off over the dump, "I knew I could do it."

"I am Violet!" she screamed at the top of her lungs as she whirled in a giant figure eight. The wind was strong up here. Her nose was cold and her ears were flat and she never wanted to stop. But if she did stop, she knew how to get going again. She dove down and curled back up again, making a perfect loop-the-loop.

Violet cut her speed. She spiraled down slowly and stroked the leaves at the top of her willow. Then she angled up toward the clouds. A hawk braked sharply and hurried away.

"Now where do I go?" Violet asked herself. "Anywhere!" she answered, and headed for the river.

Chapter Two

The sun shone and warmed her back. The river sparkled and dazzled her eyes. Violet flew low and watched the anxious crawdads scurry under the rocks. She flew high, rolling onto her side as she took the twists and turns of the river. After a while, she practiced flying on her back. She was giddy with happiness.

Mile after mile, Violet followed the shining river. The woods below her looked like a forest of broccoli, stretching on and on forever. Then suddenly, a bald patch appeared in the woods, and a faint wisp of smoke. Violet was curious. She banked sharply and landed behind a sweet gum tree.

The woods were thick here and blocked Violet's view, but she could smell the smoke. She pushed her way forward. All around her was quiet—except for the sound of twigs snapping under her feet and the sudden crash when she tripped on a vine and landed flat and hard.

She pulled herself up and leaned against an oak. Just ahead was a bright spot, an open space where no trees grew. A fire burned on a worn patch of ground. A hatchet lay on a rock beside the fire. On the other side of the fire a lopsided shed leaned into the trees. The shed looked old, a patchwork of boards and tarpaper ... but the latch on the door was new.

Violet watched, hugging the tree and holding her breath. Nothing moved and no one came. What a strange thing, to build a fire and then leave it, Violet thought. And what could be in that shed? She stared at the shiny latch on the door. Well, she thought, I know how to find out.

The door opened easily. Inside was a place to sleep: three mattresses on the bare ground and a snarl of dirty blankets. The only other thing in the shed was an orange backpack. Whatever was in it was heavy, almost too heavy to lift. She opened it up and tipped it onto its side. Out spilled a flood of hundred-dollar bills! They flowed between her legs. They almost covered her boots. When she tried to back away, she tripped and sprawled on her back. She was still lying there, feeling a little dazed, when she heard footsteps. She leaped toward the door and crashed into a small black cat.

The black cat stared at Violet. Violet stared back. He was thin—his ribs jutted out from his chest. And short. He had a fierce look, and matted lumps in his fur. He carried a carp by the gills.

17

"Someone . . ." Violet began shakily. "Someone left money in this shed."

"I did," said the black cat. He held the door open wide, and gestured with his fish. "That's mine. I stole it." His voice was proud. "From the biggest bank in the state."

Violet watched while the black cat cooked his fish. If the frying pan and the cat stood side by side, she thought, the frying pan would be taller. How could someone so short rob a bank? But he did seem to know how to cook.

"That smells good," she said.

"It won't be enough," he said.

"It won't?"

"I could eat ten of these." Sadly, he split the fish with a pointed stick and gave her a piece on a sassafras leaf. It was hot and fresh and delicious. I could eat ten of these too, she thought.

The black cat looked longingly into the pan, where there wasn't any more fish. "Oh well," he said, "come on. There's more in the river."

He led her down a faint trail to a place where the river curved. Tall sycamore trees gripped the banks with their roots and tilted into the sky. The two cats crossed the stream on a fallen tree that made a convenient bridge. Violet looked down into a deep and murky pool. She threw in a stone and a blizzard of mud rose up.

"Don't do that!" he yelled. "You'll make the snappers mad."

Violet caught up with him when he stopped beside a dying sycamore tree. Its inside was hollow. He could slip right in without even ducking his head, but she had to bend a little. There were two fishing poles inside, and a can of worms. "Here," he said, "you can use my spare."

They fished from a rock in a faster part of the stream. Violet gazed down and saw the wiggly trail of clams. How clear the water was here! The low light fell through the leaves and made patterns on the river's surface. Water striders zoomed from light to shadow. I like this place, she thought. I'm a million miles from vegetable soup. The black cat was smiling at her, a funny short smile that went with the rest of him.

"My name is Violet," she said.

"My name is Grim," he answered. "I'm sure you've heard of me. I'm a champion fisherman. I have first-place medals for every year of the Catfish Derby."

The Catfish Derby? Whoever heard of the Catfish Derby? Had anyone ever heard of it besides Grim? Violet looked at him sideways. "You may be a champion, but we're not getting any bites."

"It's the wrong time of day," Grim said quickly. "They'll bite much better at sunset."

"I won't be here at sunset," said Violet. "Can I see your medals now?"

"Oh . . . ," said Grim. "Yes. I mean no. They're lost."

Violet snorted. She reeled her line in, secured the hook, and jumped off the rock. He could go on and on about winning medals and robbing banks, but she didn't have to listen. And if it came to bragging . . . well! When he saw her take off for home, his eyes would jump out of his head.

"Where are you going?" Grim called.

"To the bridge!" she yelled back.

There was no bark left on the fallen tree bridge. It was smooth and wide and just right for Violet to sit on. She flipped her cape out behind her, dangled her feet, and stared down into the brown, silty water. If there were clams or crawdads or fish down there, she couldn't see them.

"We could try here," said a voice beside her.

"I'm all done fishing," she said.

22

Grim sat down beside her on the log. "Why do you wear this thing?" He tugged on the edge of her cape. Well, thought Violet, shall I knock his socks off? Bug his eyes out? Yes! I'll jump up right here on the log and take off—

Something pulled on her neck. She snatched at Grim and kept herself from falling, but whatever it was kept right on pulling. Violet gagged as her cape dug into her throat. She turned her head and looked down, and her eyes met the eyes of a mud-gray turtle. His jaws were locked on her cape. His shell was enormous. He was heavy enough to drag her into the water.

A knife flashed in the air. Grim pulled up on Violet's cape, taking the pressure off her throat. Then his knife cut and the fabric tore and the turtle fell—splash!—back into the pool with a hunk of purple cloth in his mouth. There was a hole now, just at the hem, the size of a big tomato.

23

"Oh no," Violet moaned. "Oh no, oh no. Now it won't work." She stood up and shook the cape out. Her precious cape, her treasure. Ruined!

"I had to cut," Grim said. "Snappers never let go."

Violet nodded mutely. She stared into the water and hated the snapper. A little breeze stirred the surface of the pool. It lifted the corners of her cape. Maybe, she thought. Maybe I still can, with the words. "I am Violet," she whispered.

Her cape billowed out in a perfect arc and lifted her gently over the river. In a rush of happiness, she soared up over the trees. She flipped onto her back. Rolled onto her side. Pointed her toes and did three cartwheels in the air. When she landed back beside Grim, his mouth was hanging open.

"The cape still works," said Violet. "Thanks."

Grim shut his mouth and nodded his head. He was speechless. She had knocked his socks off, all right.

"I'd better go home now," Violet said. The sun was falling into the tops of the sycamore trees, telling her she was late for supper. But it was hard to move. She felt deeply contented, sitting here on the log beside Grim. Maybe he bragged a little too much— but he cooked delicious fish. And when there was serious trouble, he knew what to do.

Besides, she thought, I like to show off a little myself.

Chapter Three

Things did not start out well the next day. The sun woke Violet; it was hot in her face. Her sheets were tangled. At breakfast she gagged on her egg. She fought with Dagmar and emptied a wastebasket over her head. Violet was sent to her room. And all the time it got hotter and hotter.

Violet slid under the bunk beds and lay on the cool floor. She found some old licorice there and chewed on it while she thought about Grim . . . and the orange backpack . . . and the hundred-dollar bills. When you find money, you should tell someone. A mother or father. A teacher or the sheriff. Violet frowned in the dark. But maybe this money belonged to

Grim. Maybe he was rich. That skinny cat, with the torn jeans? Rich? She remembered how he had looked yearningly into the frying pan. Could you be rich and hungry, too? Probably not.

Well then, did he steal it, like he said? True, he was short. And very thin. But he knew how to build a fire and catch a fish and deal with a snapping turtle. He had a hatchet and a knife. Maybe he *had* robbed a bank. She closed her eyes and imagined him under a bank teller's window, waving a hatchet.

The teller looked out and saw the tips of his ears. "Now little boy," the teller said, "that's not a toy—you put that away." Violet giggled. No, Grim couldn't rob a bank.

Well, if he didn't steal it, what was it doing there? Her licorice was melting away and the floor was getting hard and she really had no idea in the world how that backpack—that heavy backpack, stuffed with money—got into the shed.

"Violet, you may come out now!" Her mother's voice called from the other side of the door. Violet stayed where she was.

What if she told the sheriff about the money? Sheriff Goetschall was tall and round in the middle. He smiled a lot, and he patted her on the head when he met her outside of Lutrell's Grocery. But he wouldn't pat Grim on the head. He wouldn't smile when he saw that overstuffed backpack. He'd lock Grim up in jail. Prison. She couldn't imagine anything worse than that. No. The thing to do was to talk to Grim—if he could stop bragging long enough to explain a few things. She eased herself out from under the bed.

"Don't forget," her mother called through the door. "You need to practice your clarinet!"

Violet sighed. She really had quite a lot on her mind.

It was twelve o'clock before she could slam the kitchen door and race away through the garden. She was going to the dump, but only for long enough to get her cape from her hide-out. When she held it up to the light, it sparkled just like a dragonfly. The hole near the hem was really very small. She closed the cape quickly, with its Velcro fasteners, under her chin.

In seconds she was airborne, following the river. She would find Grim. She would settle this hokeypokey fairy-tale stuff about robbing banks. They would turn the money in to the sheriff. It was simple, really. And they might get their pictures in the *Yellow Springs News.*

Violet flew by the sweet gum tree and landed on the bridge. No sign of Grim. She checked the hollow tree and the fishing rock. She found two fishing poles and a can of worms, but

no one was casting into the stream. The fast-running river was making its usual racket, and yet it felt quiet and empty here. He must be up by the shed.

There's no smell of smoke, she thought. His fire must be dead. The heat pressed down as she followed the trail through the woods. The leaves crunched loudly under her feet. A branch cracked. All the small sounds of the forest were sharper and louder today. She stopped. Now she heard voices, coming from the clearing. She left the path and slipped from tree to tree until at last, hidden by a rough tree trunk, she could see without being seen.

There, in the middle of the clearing, three cats sat hunched over a map. Their stringy tails lay in the dirt. Their heads almost touched.

The largest of the three wore a greasy plaid shirt that didn't quite close over his belly. He waved a cigar while he talked in a deep, commanding voice. The other two looked thin, like Grim. Their ears were torn. One was missing an eye.

Plaid Shirt lifted the map and Violet saw something under it. It was orange, and all three cats had a paw resting on it. The backpack. It looked just as full as before—too stuffed to hold even one more dollar. The deep voice rose, and the big cat pointed with his cigar. Then he dropped the map and the orange backpack was covered again.

So. These mangy cats had the money now. But what about Grim? Where was he? She saw his hatchet leaning against the shed. Then her eye caught the glint of a padlock on the door. The shed was locked! A green sedan was parked by the door.

Violet shivered. Something was going on. Something that wasn't good.

Something she didn't like. What were they saying, anyway? They seemed to be arguing now. If she could just get closer!

A few feet away, a slender ash tree stretched a long branch out into the clearing. It was just what she needed. The end of the branch was directly over their heads. Violet crept slowly toward the ash, stopping behind every bush and sapling to breathe and listen and watch. A garter snake slithered over her foot. A fly sat down on her ear. She waited patiently for them to move on. Then she inched ahead.

The deep voice paused. There was the scratch of a match, the stink of another cigar, then a loud explosion of coughing. Quickly, Violet scrambled up into the ash and shimmied out on the low-hanging branch. When the coughing fit passed, she was close enough to hear every word.

Plaid Shirt was still doing most of

the talking. "Easiest job we ever did," he said. "Hardly worthy of our talents. Smallest town in the valley."

What town? Violet wondered.

"Sleepy little country bank."

Which bank? What town? What job?

The cat with one eye looked sour.

"Yeah, Rotgut," he said. "Eban Stealth robbed a sleepy little country bank, and now he's in jail. I'm not eager. I say we got enough."

"You're mistaken, Mr. Filch," said the big cat. "There is no such thing as enough." He paused, and dropped an inch of cigar ash on Filch's head. "You and Mr. Pilfer will assist me. I tell you today is the day. Two o'clock sharp is the time. Yellow Springs is the place—corner of Xenia Avenue and Short Street."

Yellow Springs! Yellow Springs was the town where she lived! Violet jerked forward on the branch and leaned out as far as she could. The branch sagged a few inches lower.

"Stick with me, friends," Rotgut continued. "I know how to plan a fool-proof job. All will be well. There will be no surprises."

Suddenly there was a crack and a loud thud. Violet landed hard, right in the middle of the map.

"Well, well, well, well, well!" The big cat grinned. He grabbed her arm and pinned it behind her back. "Wasn't it good of you to drop in on us, sweetheart. And wearing such an attractive garment." His voice in her ear was as sweet as chocolate. His warm breath stank.

"No surprises! No surprises, you say!" Mr. Filch danced with rage. "What about that snotty-nosed kid? He spills our cash all over the place. Burns five hundred dollars—just to start his fire! And now her! We could start a kindergarten."

"I'm going into third grade," Violet told him.

Mr. Filch thrust his face into hers. "I'll pull out your whiskers, kitty-poo. Every last one."

"Alas, no time! No time, Mr. Filch!" said Rotgut regretfully. "We must be on our way!"

Violet felt herself lifted in Rotgut's strong grip. She was whirled across the clearing and thrown into the shed.

Chapter Four

Violet's heart pounded. Her breath came loud and fast in the dark shed. As she got to her feet, she heard a padlock click shut. Steps walking away. Then she felt a touch on her arm.

"Violet?" said a small voice. "Is that you?"

It was Grim. She reached out and felt his fur. He was here!

It was hot and dark in the shed, and she didn't know how they were going to get out, but she had found Grim. His whiskers touched hers.

"Grim," said Violet, "you've never robbed a bank in your life. You're not a robber at all, are you?"

He shifted a little in the dark. "Well, actually, no, I'm not. What I really am—"

"That's what I thought," Violet interrupted.

"What I am really," Grim continued, "is a country-western singer. I was on my way to Nashville when you stopped by."

"You were on your way to lunch," said Violet.

"Well," said Grim, "yes. But after lunch, I was going to Nashville."

"Shhh!" Violet put her ear to the door and listened. She heard car doors slam. The ignition turning and the motor catching. The sound of the engine fading into the woods. And quiet.

"Lunch," said Grim. "We were talking about lunch. Boy, am I hungry."

Violet backed up as far as she could, dashed across the mattresses, and threw herself at the door. Nothing happened, except that her shoulder hurt.

"I wrote a song about lunch," said Grim. "Would you like to hear it?"

40

"No, I would not," said Violet. She tried a karate kick with her right foot. Nothing happened, except that her foot hurt.

"It goes like this," said Grim. He squeezed his eyes shut and howled.

"Spaghetti! With meatballs!
Macaroni! With cheese!
Pizza! Pepperoni! and anchovies, too—
And sausage, and olives,
I think that will do. . . ."

His voice trailed off into a hum. His eyes glazed over. He was lost in a warm world of food.

"Can't break down the door," Violet muttered. "It's too solid. We'll have to find a rotten board." She worked her way along the side of the shed, kicking each board. Still nothing happened, except that her toes were sore.

"Cornbread . . . and biscuits . . . and pancakes . . . ," moaned Grim.

Violet gave him a shake. "Grim! Forget about food! We've got to get out of this shed!"

"Okay." Grim sighed. "Did you say a rotten board? There's one back here."

"Now you tell me!" Violet said, as Grim pushed at a damp board in the back wall. It bent backward and let in an oblong of light. He pushed harder, and it snapped off. Grim and Violet squeezed through the ragged hole and came out behind the shed.

The orange backpack and the green sedan were gone. No one had seen the robbers drive away. No one had heard their plans or knew what town they were going to next. No one but Grim and Violet. They were the only ones who could stop this robbery.

"Come on, Grim," she said. "We're going to get the sheriff." She knew exactly how it would be. They'd warn the sheriff and he would be there waiting when the robbers walked into the bank. They'd walk right into his trap. He'd slap the handcuffs on and take them away.

Meanwhile, crowds would gather on the sidewalk. The president of the bank would step outside and call for silence. "Your money is safe," he would tell the worried customers, "thanks to Violet and Grim." Her eyes glowed as she watched the perfect picture in her head. There were her parents, gazing at her with adoring eyes while she posed for the photographers—wearing her cape, of course. There was Grim, standing beside her, his shoulders thrown back and that fierce light in his eyes. And there was Dagmar, turning a little green. It would be Violet's finest hour.

There was just one problem. How would they get into town?

She looked at Grim. He was leaning against the shed, chewing a blade of grass. "I don't think I can carry you," she said. "At least not that far." What if they had to make a crash landing in some roadside ditch? What if they fell on a power line? What if they flew too slowly and got to town too late?

"You don't have to carry me," said Grim. "We can go by log. We can start where the creek joins the river. The water's really fast there. Especially now," he explained, "after all those heavy rains. Besides, they have to stop for traffic lights and we don't."

True enough, Violet thought. There were no red lights on the river. But the robbers had a head start.

"Let's take this one," said Grim when they got to the creek. He kicked at a log that was snagged on the shore. Together they heaved it into the water. The current caught it and pulled.

"Watch out!" Violet yelled. "It's getting away!" Grim leaped on board. Violet threw herself on behind him.

The log sank under their weight and cold water swallowed her legs. Then the log bounced up again, and they raced away on the current.

Trees flashed by before she could see them. Low-hanging branches scraped her ears before she had time to duck. The river curved, and curved again. The log whirled in circles. Violet was dizzy, but she held on.

Then the river straightened itself. It grew faster. It grew louder. Limestone cliffs loomed on either side. Violet was cold. Her fur was drenched. Her teeth were chattering. She pressed against Grim. He was stiff and rigid, as though he were part of the log. The log slammed into a rock, bounced off, and hit another rock. Route 68 would have been safer, she thought. Also dryer. Her whole world had turned into water and rocks and terrible deadly speed.

Violet heard the waterfall before she saw it—a low roar that grew and

swelled until it filled the ravine. A trip down the falls would turn their log into splinters. It would grind them both into cube steaks. Could she somehow steer their log toward the shore? If she tried to fly, could her cape carry them both? Would it even work when it was wet? All these thoughts raced through Violet's head, but the river raced faster. Now she saw the smooth edge of the falls, the lip where the water curled over and dropped out of sight.

Violet jumped up. She grabbed Grim and pulled with all of her strength. His claws would not let go. The log spun around. They were going backward toward the waterfall. "Let go!" she screamed. "Violet! I am Violet!"

Then the log flipped around again and sailed over the edge, and the roar of the water swallowed everything.

Flying with Grim was awkward. He had slipped and was dangling at her side. She flew in jerks, low over the water, searching.

"There!" Grim screamed. "There's a good log!"

The new log was wider. Violet landed with a bump, Grim scrambled forward, and they sailed out into the current. The noise of the falls still pounded in their ears, but they were safe.

They raced through the dark woods and out into sunny fields, where the light was almost blinding. They whirled past the Hertzberger's barn, past towering sycamores with spotted bark, past tired cows gossiping in the shade. "We're getting close, Grim," said Violet. They passed Baily's junkyard. Slipped under a highway bridge. And ran aground by Oreford's garage.

Beyond the gas pumps Violet could see a cool arch of maples shading a peaceful street. Mrs. Gibbs was calmly pushing a stroller toward the bank.

"This is it, Grim," she said. "Here's where we leave the river."

"And find the sheriff," said Grim.

"And catch the robbers," said Violet. "Let's go."

Chapter Five

"That's cute, Violet. Did you make that for Halloween?" Sheriff Goetschall pointed to her cape. He was smiling, as usual, but he wasn't listening. Violet tried again.

"There are three robbers. They'll be driving a green sedan. They should get to the bank exactly at two." She looked up anxiously at the sheriff's clock. Only fifteen minutes left!

"That's nice, Violet. Thanks for stopping by." The sheriff stood up and stretched. "Now you better run along, honey. Your cape is dripping on my rug."

"All right, then." Violet turned on her heel. "Never mind. We'll take care of it ourselves."

"Good idea, Violet," said Grim when they stood outside on the sidewalk. "We'll take care of it ourselves." He folded his arms and stuck out his jaw. "But how will we take care of it?"

"First of all," said Violet, "we will survey the scene." She grabbed Grim's paw and hurried down Xenia Avenue toward the bank. Past the Old Trail Tavern. Past Lutrell's Grocery. Mr. Lutrell was lining up shopping carts in his brand-new parking lot. Past Deaton's Hardware. Garden tools and a shiny wheelbarrow were on display in the window.

Now they were on the corner of Xenia Avenue and Short Street. Just across from them stood a red brick building. On its doors were gold letters outlined in black.

"Miami Deposit Bank," Violet read aloud.

"We got here first," said Grim.

On the Short Street side of the bank

a new drive-through addition was going up. A cement mixer blocked the sidewalk.

"There's Larry Dillon," said Violet. "He's getting ready to pour concrete." As they watched, Larry switched the engine off, climbed down from the cab, and walked into the bank. "He's going inside to cool off, I guess. He left his keys."

She frowned as she gazed down Xenia Avenue. An eighteen-wheeler was just turning into McPhaden's Funeral Home. That looks like Fred Schickedantz with a load of coffins, she thought.

She gripped Grim's arm. "Can you drive a truck?"

"Of course."

Could he really? Or was he just making it up? It was hard to tell with Grim. Pointing to Larry's keys, she whispered her plan in Grim's ear. He nodded and cut across Short Street.

Violet jumped on a fire hydrant, chanted her words, and took to the air. There weren't many minutes left. She had to get to Fred's truck before he unloaded.

Fred had just straightened his trailer wheels and pulled into the drive when Violet landed on his hood. He slammed on the brakes, opened the door, and almost fell out. Violet flew around to the rear of the trailer.

"What are you doing?" he yelled.

"Excuse me, Fred. I'm getting the ramp down. I can't stop to talk." She lifted a latch and the doors opened. She pulled a lever and the ramp came down. She raced up the ramp and into the darkness of the trailer. She squeezed through the tightly packed coffins, all the way to the back, braced herself, and gave a shove. The casters under the bottom coffin started rolling. She gave a kick and they rolled faster, spun down the ramp, and coasted smoothly to the middle of Xenia Avenue, carrying with them a tower of heavy coffins. Fred raced after them.

A station wagon came to a stop on the other side of the coffins. The driver stuck out his head. "Watch out!" he yelled. Fred dodged just in time as two more towers came rolling down into the street. Now there was no way through in either lane.

"Not bad," said Violet. Fred groaned and tore at his hair. Violet was sorry she couldn't stop to explain, but she had to get back to Lutrell's. As she flew over the bank, she saw the green sedan pull up at the curb. Rotgut stepped out. Mr. Filch followed. They climbed the steps to the bank. She hoped she had enough time.

Mr. Lutrell was just disappearing into his store when Violet landed in the parking lot. All the shopping carts were lined up neatly. Pushing with all

her strength, she turned them around. She lined them up at the top of the parking lot entrance. One good shove, and the long column of carts raced down the incline and into the street. A horn honked angrily. Violet looked around quickly—just to make sure both lanes were blocked—and then raced on to the corner. Standing outside of Deaton's, she could keep an eye on the bank.

Mrs. Gibbs came toward her, still pushing her baby stroller. She stared up the street, where Fred Schicke- dantz was arguing with Mr. McPhaden beside a blockade of coffins. She stared down the street, where traffic was snarled behind the line of carts. Then she shrugged and stepped to- ward the curb. Violet laid a restrain- ing hand on her arm.

"Stop, Mrs. Gibbs," she said. "This is a dangerous street." She pointed, and just then the doors of the bank flew open. Rotgut and Mr. Filch raced by in a blur and threw themselves into the waiting car. The car lurched forward, then skidded to a screeching halt inches from the wall of coffins.

"Now he'll make a U-turn," Violet told Mrs. Gibbs. Sure enough, Pilfer was turning the car around right in the middle of the street. Then he roared down Xenia Avenue in the opposite direction—straight into the line of shopping carts. There was a clang and a crunch and the long line broke open and scattered over the road. Carts flipped onto their backs, onto their sides. One flew up and landed on the roof of the car. As it rolled off the windshield, Rotgut leaned over and grabbed the steering wheel.

Now the green car was backing up. Violet smiled as Rotgut turned the car and headed up Short Street. The cement mixer was right where she'd hoped it would be, backing rapidly, ready to meet the sedan. Its barrel churned around and around. Its chute swung out across the narrow street.

"Oh! Look!" Mrs. Gibbs shrieked. "That truck is empty! There's no one driving that truck!"

"Oh, yes there is," Violet assured her. "It's just that he's very short."

Just then the barrel of the cement mixer shifted and began to turn in the opposite direction. A thick stream of heavy concrete filled the street. Pilfer slammed on the brakes and grabbed the steering wheel back. Rotgut wrenched it away. The cement kept on coming. While the two of them wrestled, it sealed the doors. It covered the windshield. It buried the green sedan.

"We got them!" Violet yelled.

"Open the doors!" Larry Dillon screamed. "Get them out!"

"NO! NO!" yelled the president of the bank. "Keep them in!"

"Where's the sheriff?" Mrs. Gibbs wailed. "Somebody call Sheriff Goetschall!"

Voices swirled around Violet. "Who's the kid? Who's the little kid in the truck?" "How long before the cement gets hard?" "What's going on?"

The sidewalk had filled up with gawkers, and in seconds the getaway car was surrounded. Everyone was staring, pointing and talking, but nobody knew what to do. Violet had to take charge. She mounted the fire hydrant and spoke to the crowd.

"The Miami Deposit Bank was robbed today," she announced. "But the robbers and all of the cash are right here, under this pile of cement."

"I only went to get a drink of water," Larry Dillon interrupted. "When I got back, my truck was gone! Now I want to know who took my truck!"

"That was my friend Grim," said Violet.

Grim climbed up on the hood of the

cement truck and took a bow. Everyone cheered.

"Excuse me," said Violet when she thought they had cheered long enough, "but I think I see the sheriff coming."

Sure enough, Sheriff Goetschall was trotting up the street from the courthouse, buckling on his gunbelt. When he saw the scene outside the bank, his jaw dropped in amazement.

"The forces of law and order will take over now," Violet continued. "Our sheriff will soon have these hooligans locked up in jail."

The sheriff beamed. Everyone cheered. Then they all watched while the sheriff handcuffed the robbers together and took them away. Mr. Deaton brought shovels and brooms and the wheelbarrow from his window. Everyone rushed to scrape off the sedan and to fill the last footings before the cement got hard. Grim smoothed the tops with the side of his shovel. Violet borrowed a hose from the fire department and hosed down the street.

In the end, it all happened just the way she knew it would—only better. When all the streets were clear, when the coffins had been delivered and the shopping carts were back in their bay, the president of the bank gave a speech in their honor. The band played. Mr. Lutrell served free ice cream. Photographers were everywhere, snapping their pictures for the *Yellow Springs News.* Her parents looked amazed and happy as they stood in the crowd and watched.

Afterward, while Grim went to look for more ice cream, Violet spoke to her family. Grim could sleep in her room, in the bottom bunk, she explained. "He's very small," she said hopefully. "He won't take up much space. Besides, he can chop firewood and fry fish." She didn't mention the stolen diamonds she and Grim would

find at the dump or the raft they would build or the dangerous trips they would take on the river. Sometimes it's better not to say too much.

Violet's parents were a little surprised, but they had to admit that the bottom bunk was empty. They had to agree that she really did need someone to play with.

"But we don't have a fireplace," said Dagmar. "We don't need any wood chopped." She wrinkled her nose. "Besides, that boy is incredibly dirty."

"Well, that's easily fixed," said Grandma. "I'll just give him a good bath." And that seemed to settle it.

Grim agreed to live with Violet and her family. "Just for a little while," he said. "Just till I go to Nashville. I'm a country-western star," he told them all. "I'm sure you've heard of me. What's for dinner?"